ASTRID & APOLLO

AND THE AWESOME DANCE AUDITION

BY
V.T. BIDANIA

ILLUSTRATED BY
EVELT YANAIT

PICTU

To Siri and all the awesome Hmong dancers out there! —VTB

Published by Picture Window Books, an imprint of Capstone.
1710 Roe Crest Drive
North Mankato, Minnesota 56003
capstonepub.com

Text copyright © 2022 by V.T. Bidania.
Illustrations copyright © 2022 by Capstone.

Library of Congress Cataloging-in-Publication Data is available on the Library of Congress website.

ISBN: 9781666337440 (hardcover)
ISBN: 9781666337402 (paperback)
ISBN: 9781666337365 (ebook PDF)

Summary: Astrid and Apollo watch their cousin Lily in an amazing dance performance, and she convinces them to audition for the Hmong dance school she attends. Astrid is excited, but Apollo isn't so sure. The twins learn the audition routine and work hard to prepare for the big day. When Apollo faces a setback, he realizes how much he does want a place at the dance school. Will his creative solution save the day or cost him his chance?

Designer: Tracy Davies

Design Elements: Shutterstock/Ingo Menhard, 60, Shutterstock/Yangxiong (Hmong pattern), 5 and throughout

Table of Contents

Hi, I'm Astrid. My twin brother is Apollo, and we were born in Minnesota. We live here with our mom, dad, and little sister, Eliana.

ASTRID GAO NOU

Hi, I'm Apollo! Our mom and dad were both born in Laos. They came to the United States when they were very young and grew up here.

APOLLO NOU KOU

MOM, DAD, AND ELIANA GAO CHEE

HMONG WORDS

gao (GOW)—girl; it is often placed in front of a girl's name. Hmong spelling: *nkauj*

Gao Chee (GOW chee)—shiny girl. Hmong spelling: *Nkauj Ci*

Gao Hlee (GOW lee)—moon girl. Hmong spelling: *Nkauj Hli*

Gao Nou (GOW new)—sun girl. Hmong spelling: *Nkauj Hnub*

Hmong (MONG)—a group of people who came to the U.S. from Laos. Many Hmong from Laos now live in Minnesota. Hmong spelling: *Hmoob*

Nou Kou (NEW koo)—star. Hmong spelling: *Hnub Qub*

pa dow (PA dah-oh)—needlework made of shapes like flowers, triangles, and swirls. Hmong spelling: *paj ntaub*

tou (TOO)—boy or son; it is often placed in front of a boy's name. Hmong spelling: *tub*

CHAPTER 1

Gymnastics

"One!" said Astrid.

Apollo leaned forward.

"Two!" said Eliana.

Apollo put his hands on the floor.

"Three!" Astrid and Eliana said together.

Apollo lifted his legs and placed his feet on the wall.

He was doing a headstand!

Astrid clapped. Eliana jumped up and down. Their dog Luna licked Apollo's upside-down face. It tickled. Apollo laughed.

He felt proud! He had recently learned how to do a flip in gymnastics class. Now he could do a headstand too. Apollo put his feet back on the floor and stood up.

"Nice job! My turn," said Astrid.

"This time, I'll count," Apollo said. "Ready? One, two, three, GO!"

Astrid raised her arms and leaned her body sideways. Then she put her hands on the floor and swung her legs in the air. She put one foot down, then the other. Now she was standing up again.

"Great cartwheel, Astrid!" said Apollo.

Eliana did a forward roll. She sat up and said, "Me too!"

Astrid and Apollo laughed as Luna ran in circles around them.

Mom poked her head in from the kitchen. "Kids, what are you doing?"

"Gymnastics," said Astrid.

"Jim-nah-sticks!" Eliana said. She stood up and ran to the kitchen as Dad walked into the room. He was carrying a tall plastic cup.

"Careful!" Dad tried to move out of Eliana's way. He held the cup up high, but it was too late. Eliana bumped into him, and the icy brown drink spilled all over his shirt.

"Sorry!" said Eliana.

"What's that?" asked Astrid.

"It's Vietnamese coffee. I have to change now." Dad walked upstairs frowning.

When he came back, Apollo said, "Dad, I learned this move from a TV show. It's called the coffee grinder. Want to see?"

Just then the doorbell rang.

"Do it later. That must be Lily!" Astrid said and hurried excitedly to the front door. Their cousin Lily was visiting.

"Hi everyone!" Lily took off her shoes and followed Astrid to the living room.

"Hi Lily," said Mom and Dad. Apollo waved. Eliana smiled. Luna ran to Lily and sniffed her socks.

Lily held up five tickets. "My dance school will be in a competition this Saturday. You're all invited!"

She handed the tickets to Mom.

"Thank you!" Mom said. "That's very nice of you."

"You're welcome! A million people come watch. It's the best contest ever!" said Lily.

Apollo made a face. Surely it wasn't *a million* people. Usually, Lily liked to make things seem bigger and better than they were.

Lily saw Apollo's face. "Apollo, you'll like it, I promise. Everyone loves it, and our school always wins awards. We're called the 'Number One Dance School' for a reason!"

"What kind of dances do you do?" Dad asked.

"The school teaches Hmong, Thai, Chinese, Bollywood, and other dances too."

"That sounds wonderful," said Mom. "I loved Bollywood dancing when I was little. I also liked doing the pretty Hmong dances."

"Our teacher is an expert in all kinds of dance. We do tumbling and flips too!" Lily said.

"You do gymnastics?" Apollo asked in surprise.

"Yes!" said Lily. "A lot of dance schools do gymnastics now."

"Awesome!" said Apollo. He and Astrid smiled at each other.

"Jim-nah-sticks like this?" Eliana said as she did a forward roll and landed at Lily's feet.

Luna rolled over too. When she sat up, she wagged her tail. Everyone laughed.

CHAPTER 2

Best Contest Ever

On Saturday, Dad drove the family to the city auditorium for Lily's dance competition. Everyone crowded inside and filled up the seats.

Astrid was excited for the contest. She was carrying a bunch of white lilies to give Lily.

But Apollo wasn't as thrilled. He wished he could have stayed home to practice gymnastics.

"Found them!" Dad pointed at five seats near the front.

Astrid, Apollo, and Eliana slid into the row and sat down. Mom and Dad sat next to them.

They saved the seats in front of them for Lily's parents, Auntie Kia and Uncle Tong, and her little sisters, Gabby and Claire.

Soon the cousins arrived. "Hi!" Eliana said.

"Hi!" Gabby and Claire replied.

While Mom and Dad talked to Auntie Kia and Uncle Tong, Astrid watched the stage curtains curiously. They were closed, but she could see dancers moving behind them.

A little girl peeked out of the curtains. She had a pretty purple and green crown on her head. Sparkly gem stickers stuck to her face. She wore a bright costume with one purple sleeve. Someone pulled her arm. She closed the curtains and disappeared.

"This will be a nice contest," Mom said, reading the program.

"Don't you mean 'the best contest ever'?" Dad asked.

Astrid smiled. She couldn't wait to see the teams. "I wonder what the dances will be like," she said.

Apollo shrugged. "Lily said this won't be boring. Hope she's right!"

The lights dimmed. "Kids, it's starting!" said Mom.

Eliana said, "Wow!"

A big white spotlight shined onto the curtains. Two hosts walked onto the stage. They announced the judges and the teams. They talked about the categories in the contest. Then they introduced the first team.

Everyone clapped.

As the hosts walked off, the music started. It was soft at first but grew louder and louder. It sounded like an orchestra.

The curtains slowly opened, revealing the entire stage. Lights glowed onto the back wall, which looked like an orange sky full of puffy clouds.

"Pwetty," whispered Eliana.

Dancers ran out from both sides of the stage. Their sleeves and pants flowed behind them like scarves. They formed a big circle.

They were wearing the rainbow costumes and crowns that Astrid had seen on the girl before. They all had sparkly gems on their faces.

"Pwetty!" Eliana shouted this time.

"Shh," Dad said.

The dancers lay down on the floor in a circle. One of them stood up and danced to the middle of the circle. She leaped into the air, landed, and did a cartwheel with no hands. Everyone clapped.

The dancer kicked one leg up behind her. Then she lifted up both arms and grabbed her leg. She pulled it straight up in the air like a needle.

Apollo smiled. She looked like a scorpion he'd seen in a book!

Then the dancer put her leg down and spun like an ice skater.

Everyone clapped again. Astrid looked closely. The dancer was Lily!

"That's Lily!" she whispered to Apollo.

"I know," he said. "She's good!"

The dancers moved across the stage, pointing their toes. They swung their arms and kicked their legs high.

The best part was that they were all kids, like Astrid and Apollo!

Suddenly, the music became louder and faster. The dancers started doing flips. Everyone clapped and cheered.

Apollo's eyes grew wide. "That's cool!" he said.

After that, more teams performed. Each time a new team danced, the audience cheered. One team had all boys. They did so many kicks, turns, and flips that the audience never stopped clapping! The kicks reminded Apollo of the ones he did in tae kwon do.

Eliana was amazed by the bright colors. Astrid smiled at the pretty costumes and dance moves. Apollo clapped when the dancers did gymnastics.

Mom and Dad looked at Astrid, Apollo, and Eliana.

"Best contest ever?" Dad said to Mom.

Mom nodded. "The best."

CHAPTER 3

One Billion Hours

When the competition was over, the hosts announced the winners. Lily's team won first place. Astrid and Apollo cheered for her.

The audience stood up and clapped. Everybody had enjoyed the show.

As people walked out of the auditorium, Astrid tried to find Lily in the crowd.

"There she is!" Apollo pointed to Lily's team posing for pictures by the windows.

"Lily!" Astrid hurried over and hugged her. "Congratulations!" Astrid handed Lily the flowers.

"Thanks!" Lily looked at Apollo. "Did you like it?" she asked him.

Apollo smiled. "It wasn't *too* boring," he teased.

"So, do you want to join our dance school now? There's my teacher!" She waved at a woman nearby and said, "Teacher Yang, these are my cousins Astrid and Apollo."

Teacher Yang walked over. "It's nice to meet you! Are you twins?"

Astrid and Apollo nodded. "Nice to meet you too," they replied shyly.

"Teacher Yang, my cousins loved the dances. They said this was the best contest they ever saw! They want to try out for our school."

Astrid and Apollo looked at each other in surprise. Lily was exaggerating again.

"Wonderful!" said Teacher Yang. "Ask your parents if you can come to our rehearsal next week. We will teach a dance for the upcoming audition."

"If you get in, we can compete together!" Lily said to Astrid and Apollo.

"What?" Astrid whispered, but Lily didn't hear her.

"Do you like dancing?" Teacher Yang asked Astrid.

Astrid wasn't sure what to say. She did like dancing, but only for fun. She never danced in front of other people. She nodded anyway.

Teacher Yang smiled at Apollo. "I'm so glad you are both trying out."

Apollo didn't know what to say either, so he said, "I like gymnastics."

"Perfect! We do a lot of that. See you at our next rehearsal!" Teacher Yang waved and left to talk with other families.

Astrid was afraid to audition, but she felt like dance school could be fun. Apollo was interested in doing flips and kicks.

"Will it be hard?" Astrid asked Lily.

"Yes, you will have to work harder than you ever did before! You will need to practice for one billion hours!" Lily said.

Astrid and Apollo stared at each other, unsure.

"But it will be the most fun you'll ever have!" Lily said and clapped her hands in excitement.

* * * * *

On the drive home, Astrid and Apollo talked about the audition.

"Lily said we can try out for her dance team," Astrid told her parents.

"If we get into her school, we'll be in the dance contest next year," Apollo said.

"Sounds good," said Dad. "Is it what you want to do?"

"I want to do gymnastics," said Apollo.

"Jim-nah-sticks!" Eliana yelled.

"And I want to learn cool dance moves," said Astrid.

Mom looked back at them. "Auntie Kia told me Lily practices almost every day."

Apollo nodded. "Lily *did* say it takes one billion hours!"

Mom laughed. "Well, if you like dancing, you should try it," she said.

"We'll have to work very hard," said Astrid, thinking.

"You both are the hardest workers I know. I bet you'll be fine," said Dad.

Astrid and Apollo looked at each other. "Let's do it!" said Apollo. Astrid smiled and nodded.

CHAPTER 4

No Surprises

On the day of the audition rehearsal, Astrid and Apollo arrived at the dance school. They were wearing the dance uniforms the school required. Mom and Dad parked and walked the twins toward the building.

They passed a bubble tea shop and an ice-cream parlor. Then they saw a sign above two huge doors. It read "Number One Hmong Dance School."

Astrid took a big breath and opened the doors.

They walked down a hallway with chairs in front of a window. Parents and families were sitting in the chairs.

Astrid and Apollo tried to look in the window, but curtains inside blocked the view. Next to the window was a door that was halfway open. They peeked in and saw a big room with lots of mirrors. Blue mats lined the floor in one corner of the room.

Kids were already inside. Some looked like good dancers. Others seemed like beginners. Just like Astrid and Apollo were.

"Go ahead." Mom nodded and pointed at the door.

"We'll wait out here. Have fun!" said Dad, giving them a big thumbs-up.

Mom, Dad, and Eliana sat in the chairs by the windows. Astrid and Apollo stepped into the room.

Lily waved at them. "Hi! You're just in time. We're about to start."

Teacher Yang smiled at them. She asked all the students to have a seat on the floor.

"Welcome to the Number One Hmong Dance School! We're excited to have you here. Today I will teach you a special Hmong dance. You must learn this for your audition."

Everybody listened carefully.

"We'll practice today. Then you will go home and practice more. In one week, you'll return to try out," she said.

Astrid looked at the other kids. She couldn't wait to learn the dance. Apollo looked at the blue mats. He couldn't wait to do the kicks and flips.

"Before we begin, we must warm up," Teacher Yang said. "Let's stretch."

She showed them how to stretch their shoulders, arms, and legs. They leaned on the floor, stretched forward, and posed like frogs.

Next the students stood by the wall. Teacher Yang taught them how to reach back with their arms and climb their hands up and down the wall.

"This is a good stretch for your backs. If you're comfortable, go all the way down to a backbend," she said.

Then she took them to the mats and asked them to do cartwheels.

Astrid and Apollo smiled at each other. They had thought they might be too shy for dance school, but this was fun!

Finally, it was time to learn the dance. Teacher Yang turned on the music.

At the front of the room, she raised her arms and swayed from side to side. She danced to the beat of the music and leaped high in the air. When she landed, she leaned forward, rolled over, and slid into a split.

Teacher Yang did more dance moves. She cartwheeled across the floor. The kids watched, amazed.

Then she did a turn. She pushed her arms out and spun in a circle. She ended in a pose with her palms together in front of her chest.

Astrid and Apollo watched with big eyes. Could they do this? And how would they remember it all?

"That's the dance," Teacher Yang said. "This time, I'll go slowly so you can see each step."

The twins watched Teacher Yang dance again. They paid close attention to each step.

Then Teacher Yang said, "Now we will dance together."

The kids stood up and practiced as a group. They watched the teacher and copied each move she made.

Then they did it all again two more times.

Next Teacher Yang said it was time to work on cartwheels. She said some students might choose to do flips instead!

Everyone lined up in front of the mats. Lily was chosen to show them a flip. She ran to the mat, lifted her arms, and flipped over, landing flat on her feet.

"Remember, cartwheels are just fine too," said Teacher Yang.

Some kids did cartwheels, some practiced flips. Apollo picked a flip, since he already knew how to do it.

Next, they worked on turns.

Teacher Yang pointed her arms and kicked one leg out. She spun around in a circle.

"Looks cool!" said Apollo.

Astrid nodded.

Before long, Teacher Yang announced that rehearsal was over. "I don't like surprises," she told the students. "During the audition, do the steps just the way I showed you. No surprises!"

* * * * *

"I can't believe tomorrow is the audition already," said Astrid. She and Apollo had been practicing every day for the past week.

"It went by fast," said Apollo. It was hard work, but he was happy.

He was having fun doing flips for the dance.

Astrid had decided to do a cartwheel instead of a flip. She was great at cartwheels, and she preferred to keep part of her body safely on the ground!

Apollo yawned. He had stayed up too late the night before practicing for the audition.

Eliana was on the couch with Luna, watching. She wanted to do forward rolls with them, but there wasn't enough space in the room for all three of them to dance and tumble. So Eliana danced on the couch.

"How does my turn look?" asked Astrid.

She stuck out her arms and turned in a circle, bending one toe to the opposite knee with each turn.

"Nice, but try to go faster," said Apollo. "I still need to work on that move more. I'm going to focus on the turn tonight."

Mom and Dad walked into the room carrying food and drinks.

"Snack time!" said Mom. "The Vietnamese bakery ran out of yummy croissants, but we have these."

Dad set plates on the coffee table. "Banh mi sandwiches and bubble tea for everyone. Vietnamese coffee for me!" he said and sat down.

Eliana ran over. "Yummy!"

"Can I smell your coffee?" asked Apollo. He loved the scent of it.

Dad was about to say yes when Luna hopped off the couch and landed on his lap. The coffee spilled all over Dad.

Dad frowned. "Not again!" he said.

Mom helped wipe up the spill. Then Dad headed for the stairs to go change.

"Dad, wait! Let me show you the coffee grinder move," said Apollo.

He squatted down on the floor. Then he pointed one leg out and swung it around. When his leg got to the other side, he lifted his hand and other foot. He swung the leg behind him and back to the side.

"It does look like a coffee grinder!" Mom said.

"Nice. Wish I had some coffee to go with it," joked Dad as he went upstairs.

For the rest of the night, Astrid practiced the dance, but Apollo felt more and more tired. While Astrid worked on her turns, Apollo lay on the floor. He kept kicking his leg out like he was a coffee grinder. Soon he fell asleep. Astrid thought he was even practicing in his dreams!

CHAPTER 5

Coffee Grinder

When Astrid and Apollo got to the Number One Hmong Dance School the next day, they went to the dressing room.

Teacher Yang had provided costumes for the audition. Astrid wore a colorful Hmong skirt and a black top. Apollo wore baggy Hmong pants and a Hmong that was a little short. It showed his stomach.

Eliana poked at him. "I see your beh-wwy button!" she said.

Apollo laughed.

The twins sat nervously in the chairs by the window, waiting to be called in.

"I'll be so glad when it's over!" said Astrid. "Are you ready? You fell asleep early last night."

"I was tired from practicing the night before," said Apollo.

Each time a student finished trying out, Teacher Yang opened the door and let them out. Then she would call on the next person.

When Teacher Yang said, "Astrid Gao Nou Lee," Astrid stood up.

Teacher Yang saw Apollo. "Would you like to audition together?" she asked.

"At the same time?" Astrid said.

"Sure," said Teacher Yang.

Astrid looked at Apollo.

"I'm okay with it. Are you?" said Apollo.

Astrid nodded. "It might be more fun."

The twins walked into the room together. They looked back at Dad, Mom, and Eliana sitting in the chairs. Dad smiled and said, "Break a leg!"

Teacher Yang closed the door. "Remember, no surprises. Let me know when you're ready."

They nodded at her, and she turned on the music.

Astrid and Apollo raised their arms and moved from side to side.

They did kicks and splits, just the way Teacher Yang had taught them. They danced to the music and did all the right steps. Then Apollo did a flip and Astrid did a cartwheel. Now it was time for the turn.

Astrid stuck out her arms and pointed her toes. As she turned in a circle, she brought her foot to her knee. She spun around and around. She looked great, almost like she was spinning on ice.

Apollo was about to do the turn too, but he froze. He was ready to move his legs, but he couldn't remember which leg to point. He didn't know what to do with his arms.

Teacher Yang watched him.

Apollo's heart beat fast. Astrid finished doing the turn and posed. Teacher Yang smiled.

Apollo didn't know what to do. Teacher Yang sipped her drink and waited.

Apollo could smell the coffee from Teacher Yang's cup. He thought of Dad's coffee. He did the only thing he could remember.

He squatted down. He pointed one leg out and swung it around and around. He did the coffee grinder.

* * * * *

Astrid and Apollo sat on the floor with the other kids who had tried out, listening to Teacher Yang. She was saying the names of those who had passed the audition.

Apollo felt bad. He should have practiced the turn more, but he had fallen asleep before he could.

Teacher Yang had said no surprises, and the coffee grinder he'd done was definitely a surprise. Apollo was sure he wouldn't get in the dance school now.

Then Teacher Yang said, "And for the last two spots. I would like to welcome Astrid and Apollo Lee to our dance team!"

Apollo looked up with his mouth wide open.

Teacher Yang smiled at him. "I *don't* like surprises, but that was a good one. I do like a dancer who can think on his feet!"

Lily rushed up to hug Astrid and Apollo. "Welcome to the best dance team ever!" she said.

* * * * *

"Congratulations on getting into the Number One Hmong Dance School!" Mom said as they got into the car.

"Thanks!" said Astrid and Apollo.

"It was so fun to see you do the coffee grinder at the end," said Astrid.

Apollo let out a breath. "I fell asleep before I had a chance to practice the turn last night. The only thing I could think to do instead was the coffee grinder."

"You still looked amazing," said Astrid.

Mom nodded. "I'm sure you were both excellent."

"Thanks, but from now on, I'll get more sleep. And I won't give Teacher Yang any more surprises!" Apollo said.

Dad pulled out of the parking spot.

"How about this? Next time, practice a billion hours and rest for a billion hours too," he said.

"But first, how about we go pick up some Vietnamese coffee and croissants to celebrate?"

"I'll let the bakery do the coffee grinding this time!" Apollo said. The whole family laughed.

- Hmong people first lived in southern China. Many of them moved to Southeast Asia in the 1800s. Some Hmong decided to stay in the country of Laos (pronounced *LAH-ohs)*.

LAOS

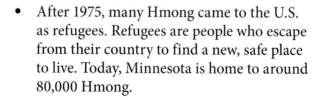

- In the 1950s, a war called the Vietnam War started in Southeast Asia. The United States joined this war. They asked the Hmong in Laos to help them. When the U.S. lost the war, Hmong people had to leave Laos.

- After 1975, many Hmong came to the U.S. as refugees. Refugees are people who escape from their country to find a new, safe place to live. Today, Minnesota is home to around 80,000 Hmong.

- Many Hmong American families enjoy outdoor activities like camping, boating, and fishing.

banh mi—a spicy sandwich filled with meat and pickled vegetables

bubble tea—a sweet dessert drink that comes in different flavors and has chewy black balls made of tapioca

fish sauce—a strong, salty sauce that is used as a seasoning for Hmong and other Southeast Asian dishes

pandan—a tropical plant used as a sweet flavoring in Southeast Asian cakes and desserts

peanut sauce—a creamy sweet and spicy peanut dip that is eaten with spring rolls

pork and green vegetable soup—pork and leafy green vegetables boiled in a broth. This is a typical dish that Hmong families eat at mealtime.

rice in water—a bowl or plate of rice with water added to it. Many Hmong children and elderly Hmong people like to eat rice this way.

Vietnamese coffee—rich coffee served with sweetened condensed milk

GLOSSARY

audience (AW-dee-uhnss)—people who watch or listen to a play, movie, or show

audition (aw-DIH-shun)—to try out for something

auditorium (aw-dih-TOR-ee-um)—a room or building used for gatherings

Bollywood (BALL-ee-wood)—the movie industry in India

category (KAT-uh-gor-ee)—a group or type

competition (komp-uh-TIH-shun)—a contest

croissant (cruh-SAWNT)—a flaky, buttery pastry

exaggerate (eg-ZAH-ger-ayt)—to overstate something

rehearsal (re-HER-suhl)—practice

scorpion (SKOR-pee-uhn)—a type of arachnid with a long tail that goes up in the back

tae kwon do (TIE KWAHN DOH)—a form of martial arts from Korea that uses movements like kicks, jump kicks, blocks, and punches

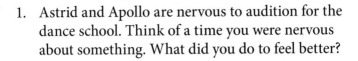

1. Astrid and Apollo are nervous to audition for the dance school. Think of a time you were nervous about something. What did you do to feel better?

2. Astrid and Apollo's cousin Lily likes to exaggerate. That means to make something sound like more than it really is. Find three times in the story that Lily exaggerates. Do you think it's okay to exaggerate?

3. Apollo realizes during the audition that he didn't prepare enough for the turn move. He took a risk by surprising Teacher Yang with another move instead. Did the risk pay off? What might have happened if Apollo hadn't taken that risk?

WRITE IT DOWN

1. Astrid and Apollo wear Hmong dance costumes for their audition. If you were in a dance audition or competition, what would you like to wear? Draw a picture or write a paragraph describing the costume.

2. After Apollo does the coffee grinder move, Teacher Yang tells him she likes dancers who can think on their feet. What does this expression mean? Can you think of other expressions that are creative ways to make a point? Write them down.

3. Lily tells Astrid and Apollo that dance school is the most fun they'll ever have. Think about the most fun you've ever had. Write a poem about how it felt.

ABOUT THE AUTHOR

V.T. Bidania has been writing stories ever since she was five years old. She was born in Laos and grew up in St. Paul, Minnesota, right where Astrid and Apollo live! She has an MFA in creative writing from The New School and is a McKnight Writing Fellow. She lives outside of the Twin Cities and spends her free time reading all the books she can find, writing more stories, and playing with her family's sweet Morkie.

ABOUT THE ILLUSTRATOR

Evelt Yanait is a freelance children's digital artist from Barcelona, Spain, where she grew up drawing and reading wonderful illustrated books. After working as a journalist for an NGO for many years, she decided to focus on illustration, her true passion. She loves to learn, write, travel, and watch documentaries, discovering and capturing new lifestyles and stories whenever she can. She also does social work with children and youth, and she's currently earning a Social Education degree.